The
Flower
of the
Realm

The Flower of the Realm

written and illustrated by EDGAR PARKER

1966
HOUGHTON MIFFLIN COMPANY BOSTON

For Carl

I

THEY MADE an odd pair — the stylish stag, proud of his antlers, and the ragged, woebegone baboon. In a tavern corner they spoke in whispers over glasses of lemonade. Outside, an autumn rain had drenched the city most of the day, but now the sun came out, as if to count the puddles, just before setting. An alley cat and a raffish beagle entered the tavern arm in arm, laughing loudly. At a center table a rooster and a horned toad quarreled bitterly over the outcome of the national hopscotch championship matches. And amid the sounds of merriment and rancor, a raccoon, wearing garters on his sleeves, played a piano licketty-split. The whisperers in the corner escaped notice.

"Nothing dishonest, you understand!" the baboon cautioned. "I may be bumping down life's ladder to the lowest rung, but I ain't stooping to crime."

"My good fellow," the stag protested, "do I look like the sort to propose anything criminal? I want your assistance in an affair of the heart — in a word, an *elopement*. The prettiest, pertest, daintiest doe in all the world has consented to be my wife. Nothing criminal at all; just a gallant, romantic intrigue! Look at it that way."

"She of age?"

"But of course. The whole difficulty is that some time ago — merely out of kindheartedness — she humored the persistent Baron Roebuck in the notion that they were engaged to be married. Merely kindheartedness, as I say. And, anyway, a spirited young doe has a right to change her mind whenever she likes, hasn't she?"

(Across the room the rooster shouted that the horned toad didn't have the brains of a katydid, and the horned toad overturned the table with a crash and clatter.)

"I got no opinions about spirited young does. They can suit themselves, I guess."

"Exactly. Now, tonight she is attending the annual ball given by the Dowager Duchess Suzanne of Scrofa. You've heard of that, surely."

The baboon nodded, drawing a newspaper from under his arm and opening it. "It says right here . . . somewhere . . . Here it is! '*A thousand candles will blaze from forty chandeliers, and . . .*'"

"I know all that; I was there last year and the year before. Now, as I say, *she* will be there tonight, waltzing round and round, never missing a step or giving any indication that her heart is pining to the breaking point for me. But it will be; no doubt about it. Now then . . ." The stag took from his vest pocket a sealed envelope.

Ignoring him, the baboon read on. "'*And if the stuffed olives to be served were placed end to end they would extend from the Straits of Gibraltar to the suburbs of Cincinnati, Ohio.*'"

"Very likely, though I'm sure no one has any such intention. Most probably they'll eat the olives and let it go at that — Will you give me your attention, Baboon? This letter . . ."

"And here it says, '*The flower of the realm will be present.*' What's that?"

"Oh, it's just an expression. The flower of the realm means the nobility — the cream of society, you might say — all the creatures of distinction and merit — *me*, for example, though this year Baron Roebuck has seen to it that I wasn't invited — which is why I need you to deliver this . . ."

" '*And the icing for the cakes would, if so applied, frost the pyramid of Cheops top to bottom!*' "

Gently the stag took the newspaper away from the baboon. "Wouldn't you like to see all this for yourself? — and to deliver this note to the doe while you're about it? I'll pay you generously."

"I can't go to the ball! I'm not no 'flower of the realm,' any way you look at it."

"Nevertheless, I have a plan. Come with me; there's no time to spare . . ."

The ball was in progress. Open windows poured forth a thumping torrent of waltzes into the night. Crouched in the damp shrubbery the stag buttoned the last button of a waiter's uniform over the baboon. "It don't fit," the baboon grumbled.

"Doesn't fit," corrected the stag.

"Doesn't fit."

"Never mind. It's very becoming, I assure you. Now take the tray of custard tarts — shoulder high, as I showed you. Yes, that's the way. And you have the letter?"

"Yes."

"Well then, it's just a question of the right moment to slip you through a window. You're to cross the ballroom, you understand, carrying the tray. No need to say a word to anybody; those who want tarts can be depended on to snatch them. When you see the doe you absolutely insist that she take a tart, beneath which you hide the note. That done, you make your way to the nearest door and — vanish!"

"And vanish?"

"Yes."

"And then you pay me?"

"Yes. Well, are you afraid?"

"A little. Mostly I feel foolish."

"Nonsense! I daresay you never looked handsomer. But *come!* The path is clear."

The window through which the baboon crawled

opened onto an empty corridor. He paused to straighten his tie and summon his courage. Then he entered the ballroom, where everything he'd read proved true: candles beyond counting — spaniels in velvet-corduroy trousers — tigresses in tiaras — and a peacock whose tail unfolded a whole galaxy of moons and stars on a blue-green sky. The baboon had never seen such gaiety and magnificence. Were these splendid creatures mere animals, like himself, with everyday troubles and concerns? "I bet," he muttered, "there's not a single flea on the lot of 'em — or only two or three at the very most!" He raised his tray shoulder high and advanced into the throng.

"Why, it's custard tarts!" cried a pekinese baroness. She'd already filled her arms with

7

cream puffs and jelly doughnuts, but she flung these into the lap of a nearby ram and set off after the baboon. "My favorite!"

"Custard tarts?" echoed the ram, dumping doughnuts and cream puffs onto the Dowager Duchess Suzanne. "Me too! mememeME!"

The duchess herself (a matronly hog) followed.

"Did I order custard tarts? I certainly don't recall it," she declared, taking four in one hoof and with the other hiding a fifth and sixth in her blouse.

"Well . . ." The baboon shrugged, embarrassed for a suitable reply. "Anyway, they're free." Then he hurried off, losing himself among the twirling dancers. Twice the doe swept past him at an alarming speed, spinning round and round in the arms of Baron Roebuck, never missing a step or showing the least sign of heartbreak. And while the baboon waited for her third circuit of the dance floor, he found his tray quickly reduced to its last tart. Not only this, but the pekinese baroness was elbowing her way toward the remaining tart with wild eyes and claws outstretched.

"You can't have it!" the baboon told her, lifting the tray out of her reach. "You've already had three."

"I can so too have it!" she retorted. "If they didn't make enough of 'em to go around it's just tee-double-oh bad for somebody else!" And she attacked the baboon's shins.

Unprepared by the stag for any such emergency, the baboon set off at a run, pursuing the waltzing doe and fleeing the custard-mad baroness.

This drew more attention than was desirable, but he couldn't help that. Dodging this way and that through the dancers, he overtook the doe only to have her decline the extended tart with a "no thank you" flung over her shoulder in passing. And away she whirled. The baboon reversed his course so as to put himself in the path of the doe and her partner on their return lap of the dance floor. But the music quickened to a whirlwind pace, carrying the dancers with it. The baron and the doe spun with dizzying abandon, faster and faster, heedless of all before them. And their collision with the baboon sent Baron Roebuck sliding on his coattails through the swinging doors into the kitchen.

Fortunately tray, doe, baboon, and tart fell in a close circle. The baboon quickly retrieved the tart, but not before a peahen, waltzing past, had stepped on it. The footprint notwithstanding, he hid the note beneath the tart and thrust it in the face of the dazed doe. "FOR YOU! I ABSO-LUTELY INSIST!" he told her with such desperate urgency that she dared not refuse. In fact, she ate it on the spot, note and all, in three nervous bites.

("That's all right with me," the baboon thought, rising and recovering the tray. "When I've delivered the goods, whether they read 'em, eat 'em, or what ain't no — isn't no — isn't any concern of mine.") The time had come to vanish.

"Ho! You there! What is this disturbance?" The duchess's steward — an enormous dog with gold-embroidered buttonholes and a long staff — approached the scene.

Seeing no path of escape open through the throng, the trembling baboon gave himself up for lost. He stood with bowed head and thumping heart, when an outcry on the far side of the ballroom brought the steward to a halt: the duchess's nose ring was missing!

"Solid gold!" she squalled. "And studded with sixteen diamonds — large as lima beans, every one of 'em!"

Of course, Constable Jowls of the Municipal Police, a hound of considerable fame, was always on hand at the duchess's balls, ready to protect the flower of the realm in any emergency. He pressed through the crowd surrounding and fanning the frantic hog.

Becoming more distraught with every word, she

assured her guests that it wasn't so much the loss of the diamonds which grieved her — "Oh no! (Pearls are my preference any day of the week.) It's the sentiment attached, y'know. The duke himself gave me that nose ring back when I was still little Suzy Porcine in *The Tiptoe Follies* — me and my sisters. 'The Dancing Dahlias,' we called ourselves. We'd come tripping out on the stage, singing, 'When it's tea-time on the trail to where I'm —' " (And she sang forth, full-throated) " '—

WAITING FOR YOU-U-U!' And there he'd be every night, first row, center — tears spurting out of his eyes every which way, just adoring and adoring me. And too shy to come right out and say so! It was his first gift, that nose ring — 'a token of his esteem,' he called it. And if that ain't — isn't — enough sentiment attached to choke a mule I'd sure like to know what is!"

Seeing the duchess so beside herself, Constable Jowls questioned instead the steward — especially about the servants: how many there were and what were their duties? And sooner or later it came to light that a stranger was in their midst, serving unordered custard tarts from a silver tray. "*Ah ha!*" said the hound. And a search began.

14

"Not yet," the young peafowl said, spreading his tail for the twenty-third time in front of the dressing mirror. He'd returned from the ball a full hour before; the hall clock was now chiming two-in-the-morning; his valet stood by, wearily extending his night robes. "Not yet. I'm not sleepy."

The bird had come of age the preceding spring. This dazzling expanse of tailfeathers, for which he'd yearned throughout a seemingly endless childhood, was his at last. And, having just attended his first ball at the Scrofa Palace, he was giddy with glory. "Believe me, Herschel," he told the patient valet, "when I danced the pavane everyone withdrew from the floor and gazed in breathless admiration. And there were three peahens present — heiresses all — who positively made fools of themselves over me!" He took a backward step, shifted himself a bit to the left, and for the twenty-fourth time erected his tail. *"Simply lovely!"*

Then it happened: one long, glittering feather separated itself from the array and glided silently to the floor. The peacock regarded it for several moments in stunned disbelief. Then he raised his

eyes to the valet, clearly
demanding an explanation.

"Well, it's starting, sir,"
Herschel replied.

"What's starting?"

"Your winter molt."

"I beg your pardon!"

"Shedding, sir. Losing your tail."

"*Loo-oo-oosing* . . . my TAIL!

I've only just got it. You can't be serious!"

"But of course, sir — every year. Surely you expected this. Surely you've observed your elders molting!"

"No . . . Yes, I've seen miserable, snaggled tails before, but I'd supposed this was due to disease — old age — negligent grooming — something like that. I never thought it would happen to MEE-E-E! I've waited all my life for this tail!" In his agitation, another long feather dislodged itself and drifted — greens, blues glistening in the candle-light — to the floor. Again the peafowl stared in dismay.

Herschel attempted a pursuasive smile. "Next year you'll grow another — maybe even more magnificent."

"You mean they're all to fall out — *all?*"

"The sooner the better, I'd say, once they've started. Haven't you seen peacocks going about with two or three bedraggled . . ."

"Yes, I told you I'd seen 'em. But not me! Nonsense! Go bring the glue pot, Herschel. And paper clips! And gummed tape! And string! And . . ."

The doorbell rang, startling the peacock as if

a cannon had blasted. "I'm at home to no one! No one! No matter what!" Snatching up the fallen feathers, he fled behind a screen.

The valet lit a spare candle and, shielding the flame with a paw, descended the stair. At the door he was greeted by the blinding glare of a lantern in his face. A hound and a fox, introducing themselves respectively as Constable Jowls of the Municipal Police and his deputy, apologized for the late hour of the visit. In very loud whispers, such as nearly blew out the valet's candle at every word, Constable Jowls recounted how a baboon, masquerading as a waiter at the ball, had stolen the duchess's nose ring — evidently making his escape across the banquet table. "Because," the hound explained, "he seems to have stepped in the cream cheese and horseradish dressing with one foot and the strawberry jam with the other."

"Alternating tracks of which," added the fox, "have led us, while they lasted, into this neighborhood. Have you seen or heard anything strange?"

Herschel shrank back in the doorway. ". . . No!"

"Perhaps the peacock . . . ?"

"Nothing, I assure you. Anyway, it's impossible to question him tonight. He has retired, much fatigued."

"Tomorrow then. Meanwhile see that the doors and windows are bolted. Again our apologies, and good night."

Herschel bounded up the stairs. Trembling with excitement, he announced the news. "The Dowager Duchess of Scrofa has been robbed, and . . ."

Wild sobs answered him from behind the screen. "I *know* all that, Herschel! Don't try my patience at a time like this! *The glue! String! Tape! Wire!* . . ."

On the roof of the peacock's house, curled up in the recess of an attic window, the baboon lay, panting in exhaustion. Moreover, it was long past his bedtime; his eyelids drooped heavily. "Well, baboon," he told himself, "you're a fugitive from justice! Not even no ill-gotten goods to show for it either." Thoughtfully he raised a foot aloft and scratched it. "— Not even *any* ill-gotten goods . . . Aw, what's the use improving your grammar; what's the use of anything! You're a all around failure. Give up, baboon! Quit the struggle!" Slowly the heavy lids blinked; slowly the well-scratched foot sank back to its place on the windowsill. He yawned, making a generous display of teeth. "Good night, baboon!" The silver tray slipped from his grasp and fell silently

through the night air . . . silently until it struck Constable Jowls of the Municipal Police. And then all manner of noise resounded from the street below.

The fox, recognizing the missile as a silver tray, shouted for assistance in the chase. The hound moaned and wailed, announcing to the world that his hat was crushed beyond repair and his head very likely so too. And as the beams of lanterns flashed upward among the eaves, the baboon took flight across the rooftops.

"How's your head?" the fox asked.

The constable's head was none the worse. But after the bellowing he'd done — after swooning twice in public, he thought more was expected of him than a slight bruise. So he'd remained at home for four days and returned to work wearing a new hat and an unnecessary bandage. "— As well as could be expected," he replied to his deputy. "Now get out of my chair. How goes the case of the duchess's nose ring?"

There were two ways of looking at it, according to the fox. He'd found on investigation that the duchess was forever reporting losses to the

Lost and Found Bureau (one croquet mallet in good condition; one mouth organ, tooth-marked; one ebony back-scratcher, much used). And he'd had a heart-to-heart talk with her grace's steward who confirmed that the hog was both careless and forgetful; her croquet mallets and mouth organs were usually found behind the sofa cushions or tangled in the bed sheets. "And so might the nose ring," concluded the fox. "That's one way of looking at it."

"But the baboon . . .?"

"Yes, the baboon. Clearly he was up to mischief. But not only he! When I returned to question the peacock the next morning, he'd disappeared without a trace. And not only he! Baron Roebuck vanished two days later. Both he and the peacock attended the ball, so either had access to the duchess's nose ring. Then there's Sir Stephen Stag, who is known to have been resentful that he wasn't invited to the ball this year. *He* (according to a not too reliable alley cat) was seen in the company of the baboon in a tavern of rowdy character on the very day of the ball. Perhaps he was bent on revenge. In any case, he too . . ."

"Has disappeared?"

"Quite. So you see, with such suspicious behaviour left and right, perhaps the nose ring was actually stolen. That's the other way of looking at it."

"And you have no clues as to the whereabouts of the baron, the peacock, the stag, or the baboon?"

They weren't in the city; the fox was certain of that. "We've searched high and (as regards the baboon) low. But Herschel (the peacock's valet, you know) has been seen, re-entering the peacock's house. On receiving this report, I hurried there just in time to see him sneaking out with a satchel, containing (insofar as could be observed) a pair of corduroy bedroom slippers and a backgammon board. He fled the instant I hailed him."

"Surely you pursued him!"

"As far as the bicycle path in the woods."

"And then?"

"Why, then it was *suppertime*, for goodness-sake! I came home, of course. But, judging from the direction of his flight, I suspect that the peacock is in hiding at a secluded, rustic inn by the name of Hollyhock Haven, located just beyond the old dueling grounds in the woods."

"I've heard of it. A den of thieves, no doubt." The hound, city-born, city-bred, distrusted the countryside and all who frequented it.

"On the contrary, Constable, Hollyhock Haven is quite a stylish resort for animals who want to get away from it all."

"From *what* all? From civilization — from law and order, that's what!" The hound pressed his paws to his furrowed brow. Then with a heavy sigh he rose. "Come along, Fox. Our duty lies before us — however dismal the path! however horrid the destination! however outnumbered we be by fiends waiting in their lair!"

"Should we take our overshoes, do you think?"

II

BIRDS TWITTERED in every tree and bush. Crickets hopped about, deliriously happy, among the weeds. "Fools!" the hound snorted. Swatting wildly at swarms of midges, he preceded the fox along a rocky, overgrown lane. "Nature is all very well in its place; and its place, if you ask me, is in a pot on a windowsill. No one with a clear conscience would venture where the pavement ends."

Midway across the bicycle path, only a timely lunge saved the constable from being run over by the pekinese baroness, pedaling past at high speed, smartly dressed in a black bowler hat and trailing veil. "Careless, careless," she commented, never

turning her head as she vanished through the trees. "— careless, careless, careless . . ."

The fox assisted the hound to his feet and brushed his jacket. "Now, Constable, we're coming to a stretch of woods much favored by strolling lovers."

There was no escaping the fact; the barks of ancient trees testified to it in countless carvings of arrow-pierced hearts and coupled names. " 'The gander loves the goose,' " Constable Jowls read on a gnarled oak. And a nearby maple informed him that "the goose loves the gander." "Well, that's nice!" he said — the first indication of approval he'd given since leaving the city. If he had examined the grove more closely, he'd have learned that "Freddy Fawn loves the doe" — "Baron Roebuck loves the doe" — "Cyril Cerf loves the doe" — as did many, many others. But the hound didn't linger. "What's this clearing in the trees ahead?" he asked his deputy.

"The old dueling grounds where formerly the cream of society settled their rivalries."

"Terrible! Terrible! Glad all that stupidity has been long since outlawed." The words were scarcely out of his mouth when, entering the clearing, he found the weeds freshly crushed underfoot and a huckleberry bush trampled to splinters. Deep hoofprints pocked the earth. *"A duel!"*

The fox was forced to the same opinion. "Whom do you suspect?"

Constable Jowls knelt and studied the tracks through a magnifying glass. *"Ungulates,"* he muttered. *"Artiodactylous ungulates."*

"Oh, foreigners!"

"Not at all. I merely stated that the duel was fought between hoofed animals with an even number of toes."

"Sir Stephen Stag and Baron Roebuck!"

"My thoughts exactly. One slain, the other in hiding! Grim doings, fox! *Murder! . . ."*

A wail of agony sounded from the distance ahead, chilling the hound and the fox to the marrow of their bones.

"Come along, fox — however horrid the destination! however outnumbered we be by fiends waiting in their lair! Which way lies Hollyhock Haven?"

"Hollyhock Haven!" It wasn't the fox that answered, but a kangaroo, stepping from behind a laurel bush with a basket under his arm. "Good

morning, gentlemen. Let me introduce myself:
I'm the proprietor of Hollyhock Haven — out
gathering pecans for fudge. If you're bound for
Hollyhock Haven, let me conduct you. Are you
coming for lunch? — or longer? I'm afraid I have
only one room available, if you don't mind shar-
ing. Lucky there's a vacancy at all, in fact. When
I opened the inn, everyone told
me, 'No, no; you must build
an inn on the highway,
preferably at a
crossroads.' But
I said to them,

'You'll be surprised,' I said, 'at the many animals who want to get away from it all now and then.' And, as it turns out, even *I'm* surprised!"

"Sir," the hound said sternly, "I am Constable Jowls of the Municipal Police, and I'm in considerable doubt that your inn is an honest place."

The kangaroo was taken aback. "Why, there're no hollyhocks about; I admit it! In naming the inn I was simply carried away by the aitches."

"I'm not speaking of hollyhocks, but of fugitives from justice. I say your inn is the haven of thieves and murderers!"

The kangaroo denied this vigorously and said, furthermore, that he was mistaken about a vacancy. "There's no room whatever, after all. I apologize for having misled you. Good day, gentlemen."

The officers followed close at his heels. "What was that awful cry a moment ago? Did it come from Hollyhock Haven?"

"It did," the kangaroo admitted. "A pathetic case! truly touching! A young peacock, closeted day and night in his room, is shedding his tail for the first time — perfectly natural this time of year. But he refuses to look at it that way; to him it's the end of the world. Ah, youth! youth! Every time a feather falls he shrieks. Bad for business, I can tell you! But I'm a sympathetic soul — compassionate to a fault, I am. And, after all, he's paid in advance for his room till spring. In any case, he's neither thief nor murderer. So you can look elsewhere."

"Kangaroo, a duel was fought in these woods quite recently — a duel of such ferocity that you cannot have been ignorant of it!"

"I knew nothing of it beforehand, I promise you."

"But afterward?"

"I'm compassionate to a fault."

"*Oh ho!* The murderer's paid in advance for his room, has he!"

The strains of an accordion began to be heard, pumping a polka onto the forest breeze. A few steps more and Hollyhock Haven appeared through the foliage. Even Constable Jowls would have had to admit that it was an inviting place. "What do you know of the duel, Kangaroo? And no more fiddle-faddle evasions!"

"Because," added the fox proudly, "we already know more than you think we do. We know

who did it. *Artio–?* You tell him, Constable."

"*Artiodactylous ungulates.*"

"No one here registered under that name," the innkeeper said positively. He dashed ahead and barred the door with his outstretched arms. "Have you a warrant to enter and search?"

The air pulsed with the rollicking polka. "I'd ever so much like a raspberry soda," the fox told his superior. "Make up with him, so he'll serve me a raspberry soda."

"Don't be frivolous, fox. We're concerned with *murder!*"

"But I'm *thirsty!* It's been a long walk," he whimpered. "Supposing I *di-i-ied* for want of a raspberry soda; *then* you'd be sorry, and it'd be practically the same as murder!"

The kangaroo was moved. "You can come in (assuming you can pay). But not he!"

"Well, if it comes to that," said the constable, "*I'm* thirsty too."

"You're taking advantage of me, Constable!" the innkeeper charged. "I won't have you disturb the privacy of my guests."

"*I want a raspberry soda!*" the fox wailed, stamping his feet.

Overhead, in an upstairs chamber, the peacock screeched, blasting his anguish through the forest a half mile in every direction.

"My heavens!" exclaimed the cringing hound. Even the polka faltered.

"Bad for business," the kangaroo muttered, shaking his head. "Bad for business."

The door that the kangaroo was shielding opened behind him, and Herschel appeared, large tears brimming his eyes. "He's so cross! Morning to night I get nothing but harsh words."

The kangaroo told him never to mind and took out a handkerchief to wipe the valet's tears. "Look on the bright side; you can lick the bowl when I make fudge this afternoon!"

Herschel looked on the bright side and smiled.

Constable Jowls slipped past the kangaroo and entered the inn.

Atop the reception desk the hotel register lay in full view. The hound bent over the pages and ran a paw down the list of guests.

"Won't do you any good," the kangaroo called from the doorway. "Animals seeking seclusion almost never give their real names. For example, the peafowl upstairs in room 2-D has registered as a penguin."

"Well, if he's trying to keep his molting a secret, you might suggest that he leave off that hollering."

"Constable, I should caution you against meddling in the affairs of my guests, many of whom are very important personages, influentially connected with king and court. Now that you've been warned, come — I myself will introduce you to the guests. Better that than have you sneaking and prying."

The kangaroo led Constable Jowls to a sunny courtyard where various animals sat at tables under a wisteria arbor. Waiters, bearing refreshments, moved about over the flagstones. Behind a trellis of climbing roses the accordionist made his music.

"This is Mr. Caretta," said the kangaroo at the side of a loggerhead turtle, staring into space and clutching a lap robe. "He's somewhat deaf and very, very old; no one knows how old for sure — well over a century though. He even remembers the great auks, which have been extinct for ages — TELL THIS GENTLEMAN ABOUT THE GREAT AUKS, MR. CARETTA — MR. CARETTA, DO YOU HEAR ME?"

The turtle blinked to life. "Cream and sugar both, thank you, but not too much of either."

"TELL THIS GENTLEMAN, MR. CARETTA — WEREN'T YOU FAMILIAR WITH THE GREAT AUKS?"

The turtle devoted several seconds to making

GREAT AUK

rasping noises and blinking his eyes before replying, ". . . Not overly . . . no sirree . . . Smelled
of sardines, they did, every one of 'em."

"THANK YOU, MR. CARETTA." The

innkeeper and the constable turned to the next table — where no introduction was needed; the fox, halfway through his second raspberry soda, released the straws long enough to pay them a happy grin.

At the adjoining table sat a bobcat with his collar open at the throat and an expression of poetic suffering on his face. He rose and introduced himself. "My name need not be disclosed (noble and renowned though it be). Whence I come and whither I wander cannot concern you. But I can tell you briefly why you find me here. Two years have passed since fate first brought me into these regions and caused me to lose my heart to the fairest lady-bobcat that ever graced the fork of a tree. My days flowed as in a radiant dream until circumstances (which I shall not reveal) tore me from my happiness and sent me into foreign ports. I left with a vow on my lips to return and claim my promised bride. Now, after undergoing such adventures as I daren't breathe utterance to, I have returned to my beloved . . . Only, for the life of me! I can't recall her name or address. But *this* I do recall: I whittled that sweetest of names into the branch of a sycamore. For three con-

secutive nights have I roamed the grove, perusing by guttering candlelight sycamores, trunk and bough. Then yestereve, as some distant tower tolled the midnight, a gust of wind extinguished my candle, and there came to me, as in a vision, the very spot where stood the tree on which I carved the name of my beloved. By lurid moonlight, I made my way feverishly to the remembered scene, and . . ."

The peacock's wail rent the air, addling the accordionist and waking Mr. Caretta. "— cream and sugar both, thank you, but not . . ."

"*Go on! Go on!*" The hound seized the bobcat's shoulders. "What did you find at the remembered scene?"

"A stump! The stump of my sycamore!" He sat down and lowered his face into his arms.

"Hey! Hey! Musician! Get back to playing!" The kangaroo clapped his hands sharply. "*Something jolly*, and none of this lagging! Remember you're hired only on trial." As the accordion wheezed to life again, the kangaroo explained to the hound, "My regular musician, a gypsy-coyote fiddler, resigned yesterday, nerves completely shattered by the peacock's shrieks. Ah, the ordeals of innkeeping!" He now led Constable Jowls to the table where sat two "very important personages" — none other than Baron Roebuck and Sir Stephen Stag, their heads bowed awkwardly over the table-top, their antlers hopelessly interlocked.

"*Ah-ha! Ah-ha!*" cried the constable. "This is what comes of flouting the law and behaving like simpletons!"

"We know it, we know it, we know it," the two muttered in unison.

"Do you dare deny," the hound demanded, "that you've been dueling?"

"Nothing could be more obvious," the stag sighed impatiently. "Don't be tedious, Constable.

39

Baron, could we now face the other direction again? I'm getting another crick in my neck."

"But of course, of course. And do please call me Buck, won't you?"

"Why, yes, Buck. And you must call me Stevie." Slowly, painfully the two deer altered their position and turned their backs to Constable Jowls.

"Oh no!" he cried, running to the other side of the table. "You shan't get away with breaking the law as lightly as that."

"My dear constable," said the baron. "Can you seriously say that we're getting away with anything lightly? You see before you two gentlemen paying dearly for their folly. Do you realize that we must remain in this absurd connection till the annual shedding of our antlers?"

The kangaroo was offended. "I must say, Baron, that a luckier and more ungrateful pair of deer never lived. Do you think you're the first to have entangled your antlers? Most deer in your plight perish from starvation and vexation and exhaustion and exposure. If Hollyhock Haven had not been nearby and if I hadn't come to your assistance, where would you be now? I ask you."

"We're indeed fortunate, Kangaroo. You have preserved us from public ridicule as well as those other things. We thank you and acknowledge our debt, which is daily reckoned in dollars-and-cents and duly paid — Stevie, my lad, be so good as to shift our postures again; my right leg is becoming numb." Slowly, awkwardly the duelists rearranged themselves, turning their backs on the innkeeper and the constable — who circled the table and confronted them again.

"Constable," said the stag, "cease persecuting us. We have learned our lesson in every way. The heartless, fickle beauty over whom this gentleman and I threatened each other's life has — according to the society pages of the morning paper — eloped with a lieutenant colonel of the Palace Guards. Ah, Buck, perhaps our greatest fortune has been to escape this cruel flirt, this ballroom butterfly!"

"Assuredly. She proved wholly unworthy of us. Never again will long lashes and a slender ankle bewitch me. Do you know what I shall do, Stevie? I shall find me a substantial, responsible, intelligent mate, past all the giddiness of youth — a good, plain, stout doe who knows her way around the kitchen."

"I too! Exactly."

"*Exactly? . . .* Well, in that case, Stevie, believe me, if we should fix our fancies on the same one, I'll gladly give her up to you. The sort I have in mind is in plentiful supply."

"No, no, Buck, I insist! If we should address ourselves to the same good, plain, stout doe, who knows her way around the kitchen and is past the

giddiness of youth, you must permit *me* to withdraw. No, no, we'll have no dispute!"

"*No dispute ever again!*" said they both together with such emphasis as to upset a teacup, which shattered on the flagstones — "Put it on the bill, innkeeper," the baron moaned. It wasn't the first crockery the clumsy pair had broken.

"Gentlemen," said Constable Jowls, "I shan't arrest you — for two reasons. First, I don't think the law can impose a more apt punishment than that which you have brought upon yourselves. Second, I fear you'd be extremely awkward and troublesome prisoners to maintain until you've shed your antlers. The innkeeper is welcome to the task, and I hope he charges you plenty for it!"

The fox, having quenched his thirst, having licked his lips and observed the goings-on with great interest, now joined his superior. "Well, Constable, now that we've solved the disappearances of the peacock and the two deer, that leaves only the baboon as the thief of the duchess's nose ring."

"*Baboon!* did you say?" asked the kangaroo, plainly alarmed.

"*Baboon!*" repeated Constable Jowls. And the polka ceased abruptly. Nothing but an intense silence came from the trellis of climbing roses.

"I . . . I . . . I engaged a strange baboon this very morning," confessed the kangaroo. "To replace the gypsy fiddler. I know nothing whatever of his character; he could furnish no references. If you'd like to question him, he's there behind the trellis — *Hey there! Musician!*"

No one answered. No one was to be found behind the trellis. "Quickly! Surround the grounds!" Constable Jowls shouted to the fox and the kangaroo. And the three of them bounded from the courtyard.

The bobcat sobbed into the cradle of his arms. Mr. Caretta stared into space. The stag and Baron Roebuck agreed to another change of posture. And the baboon, having circled the inn, re-entered unnoticed. He climbed the arbor overhead and vanished into an open window.

"Stevie, my lad," said the baron, "be a good chap and scratch behind my left ear. I can't quite reach the spot."

And Stevie was a good chap and did so.

"A little higher. Yes, that's the place."

The kangaroo returned through the inn door. The police officials rushed into the courtyard from opposite sides. "He must be hiding inside!" the hound declared. "Kangaroo, have you the master keys?" Without a pause for breath, they leaped through the inn door. To the tramp of feet, the jingle of keys, and the slamming of doors in swift succession, the search proceeded throughout Hollyhock Haven.

Mr. Caretta stirred. "Has the music stopped?" he rasped. But no one answered.

"Do you know any riddles, Buck?" the stag asked. "It might help to pass the time."

The baboon re-emerged from the window and crawled over the arbor. "*Stag! Stag!*" he hissed loudly.

With the baron's cooperation the stag looked upward among the wisteria vines. "Oh, it's you, Baboon. I trust you don't expect to be paid. The doe is quite out of my life — and good riddance, too!"

"Sir, please tell the constable I didn't break into the ball to steal the duchess's nose ring!"

"*There he is!*" the kangaroo cried, peering out a window.

"Oh, sir!" the baboon pleaded. "*Tell them! Tell them!*"

The officers and the innkeeper dashed out onto the courtyard. "I'm sorry, Constable," said the stag. "I cannot possibly be held responsible for the baboon's conduct at the ball. It's true that I engaged him to deliver a note, which I repent heartily. He seemed, though down and out, a reasonably honest fellow. I had no part in his thieving; indeed he abused my confidence shamefully. And I will give you every assistance (within the limits of my present inconvenience) in bringing the scoundrel to justice."

"*Stag!*" cried the baboon, wagging a finger down through the arbor, "if you're among the flower of the realm, I'm glad I'm a weed!"

"After him!" the constable shouted. But neither the kangaroo nor the fox were skillful at climbing. "Well, bring a ladder, for goodnessake!"

The kangaroo brought a ladder. The fox mounted it. "But let me say this, Constable!" he called down from the upper rungs. "I'm not sure the baboon's guilty a bit."

"Catch him, idiot!" replied the hound, "or you're fired!"

The baboon fled the arbor and deftly scaled a drainpipe to the roof.

"But the arbor's shaky!" complained the fox, creeping warily over the beams and vines. "And, anyway, the baboon must come down by himself sooner or later."

Constable Jowls told the deputy to make the arrest forthwith or resign from the force.

"I'll bite!" the baboon shouted from the highest peak of the roof. Then, as a show of defiance, he lifted the accordion and resumed the polka. But tears streaked down his cheeks, and he stopped playing. ("What's the use, Baboon! Give up! In prison you'll be fed, you'll have a cot to sleep on and a roof over your head.") But he didn't surrender. He remained where he was, sniffling and blotting his tears on his knuckles.

The fox crept back to the ladder. "Didn't you hear him, Constable? He'll BITE!"

"So will I, Fox," Constable Jowls snarled, "if you come down without him!"

"Well, if it comes to that," declared the fox in a fit of rebellion, "so will I!"

"*Are you threatening your superior?*"

Rebellion gave way to despair. The fox too began to cry.

"No, no, Fox," the baboon called. "I'll come

down. As you say, I'd have to anyway, sooner or later."

All eyes were following the descent of the baboon when the Duchess of Scrofa entered on a bicycle — pedaling with remarkable grace in spite of her weight, and wearing her nose ring. "Constable!" she giggled. "I have the *funniest* thing to tell you! Really the *funniest!* I've just had the queen over for lunch (her birthday's tomorrow, y'know). And I served her an upside-down cake, and . . . well, let me go back a bit. I guess I just dropped the nose ring at the ball. And then probably the waltzers kicked it around some. And then somehow it got into the kitchen — maybe along with Baron Roebuck, y'know. And then . . . well, it wound up getting baked in the upside-down cake I served her highness at lunch today. It was *too* funny, really! You see, the queen was chomping away when, as the steward puts it, she 'struck gold.' And she thought it was a party favor, y'know. And *believe me!* we had quite a scrap, we did, before she'd give it up. 'Course I told her about all the sentiment attached, y'know, and I let her take home the butter knife instead, so it was all all right. And, well . . ." She tossed her snout about, displaying the ring. "Here it is!" There it was, fourteen-carat gold, studded with seven diamonds the size of mustard seed.

"I told you, didn't I?" the deputy said, descending the ladder.

The constable mumbled that he was only doing his duty. "And the stag here said . . ."

"Sir Stephen? — Oh Constable," the duchess laughed, "don't rely on Stephen. I've known him since he was a fawn. Got good enough manners, I guess, but most of what he has to say isn't worth a slice of mud pie. Y'know what I mean; he's sort of flighty — Aren't you, Stephen?"

"Never you mind what they say, Stevie," the baron consoled his companion. "I mean to think the very best of you until we shed our antlers. And you must do the same for me. Or else goodness knows how we'll manage!"

The baboon grabbed the accordion and began squeezing out the polka with such fervent joy that it sounded like a hymn of thanksgiving.

"I'm afraid I've caused a lot-lot-lot of trouble, haven't I, Constable!" the duchess said. "And I want to make it up to everyone. To begin with . . ." She turned to the kangaroo. "Let's have a party here this very evening at my expense! And let's let that poor, mistreated baboon be the guest of honor!"

And so it was.

Lanterns and garlands of autumn leaves were strung about the arbor. In the middle a log fire crackled and blazed, over which the guests roasted marshmallows.

Mr. Caretta, staring into space, lost interest in his marshmallows and let three in a row burn to a crisp. "MR. CARETTA," yelled the innkeeper, "TELL HER GRACE ABOUT THE OLD DAYS!"

"The *what?*"

"THE OLD DAYS!"

The turtle gave the duchess a bewildered glance. "Any particular old day? There've been an *awful* lot of 'em, you know!" — which was perfectly true, so the question was abandoned.

The door to the inn opened, and the peacock, making his first public appearance since he'd registered at Hollyhock as a penguin, joined the party. On his tail (or rather where his tail had been) he wore a tasteful arrangement of artificial flowers and

bows of ribbon, which Herschel had created. "I apologize to everyone for having behaved so sill-ily," he announced. "I have attained maturity through grief and suffering. I have come to realize that vanity is idle and that outward beauty is noth-ing, nothing at all. I shall devote myself hencefor-ward to improving my mind." (He carried — rather conspicuously — a large volume entitled

How to Become a Wizard at Ticktacktoo, in Twelve Easy Lessons. "You see, I've learned the most important lesson in life — *humility!* And with the coming of next year's spring I shall re-emerge in society a changed creature. My humility will positively stagger you with admiration! And if that doesn't, my improved powers of mind will. And if that doesn't, surely the combination of stunning humility, intellectual brilliance, *and* the magnificent new tail I shall have grown will set the whole town talking of nothing else!"

"So much," grinned Herschel, who'd received an enormous raise in salary, "for the idleness of vanity!"

"Oh, it's so nice," said the Duchess, "when everybody's happy!" And everybody was — more or less — except the stag, the baron, and the bobcat.

"Has the music stopped?" asked Mr. Caretta.

"Yes," the guest of honor replied, slipping the straps of the accordion over his shoulder. "But I'll be glad to play. Any old favorites?"

"Do you know," asked the duchess, " 'The Susquehanna Holiday'?"

"*Do* I know 'The Susquehanna Holiday'!" the

baboon exclaimed, rolling his eyes, capering, and swelling the opening strains from the accordion. The duchess leaped to his side and joined him in a duet, miming with appropriate gestures the words as they sang:

Floating down the Susquehanna
   on a TWO
   BY
   FOUR,

With no rudder other than a
  Broken OAK-
  EN
  OAR!
We'll embark at O-ne-onta
Undiscouraged by the fact
That we shortly will confront a
  Roaring CAT-
  A-
  RACT!
To a twangy ukulele
  I will SING
  OF
  LOVE,
While I spurn mosquitoes gaily
  With a FRIEND-
  LY
  SHOVE.
We will paddle to Towanda
(Isn't *that* a pretty name!)
With an empty pocket and a
  Bosom FREE
  OF
  BLAME!

Aren't we happy! Isn't this a
    Capti-VAY-
    TING
    SONG!
If you wait at Catawissa
    You can COME
    A-
    LONG!
Floating down the Susquehanna
    On a TWO
    BY
    FOUR,
With a bit of luck we can a-
    Rrive at BALT-
    I-
    MORE!

To the ensuing applause the duchess frisked
about. "I haven't felt this rambunctious in I
couldn't tell you how many years! — Or I *could*
maybe." She slapped the turtle on the back.
"Couldn't we, Grandpappy! But we *won't!*"

"Cream and sugar both, thank you, but not too
much of either."

"BARBARA!" cried the bobcat, his eyes ablaze

with the reflected flames of the logs into which he seemed about to hurl himself. "That's *she!* Don't you see? BARBARA!"

And they looked and they saw: carved on a log, newly thrown on the glowing heap, was an arrow-pierced heart proclaiming that "Baron Byron Bobcat loves Barbara."

"I remember it all now!" he shouted. "Two-eleven Poinsetta Boulevard, apartment 4-G." And he fled into the night.

"He should have taken a guttering candle," the fox suggested.

"He'll find the way," said the kangaroo.

"Oh, isn't it nice," the duchess squealed, "when everyone's happy!" (And so they were — except the stag and Baron Roebuck.) "Baboon, I *need* you! I'll put you on my payroll just to sing the old songs with me."

But the baboon gazed soberly into the burning logs.

"Well, tell me then," she insisted, "exactly what you want out of life?"

"You'd laugh."

"I won't, I promise. And I promise to see that you get it."

"Well . . . I'd like a newsstand concession on the corner of Seventh Avenue and Terrapin Square."

"*You shall have it!* And it'll be the grandest newsstand that ever was. And I'll buy all my papers there."

"So shall I!" said the fox.

"We too!" cried Herschel and the peacock.

"And I guess I will too," Constable Jowls agreed.

Baron Roebuck had fallen asleep, his head forcing that of his companion as well to the tabletop. The baron's dreams being moderately entertaining, now everyone was happy but the stag. As the baron's thunderous snoring outraged the stag's ears and set their interlocked antlers to vibrating, the stag shuddered, "Heaven give me patience!"

EPILOGUE

THE READER might like to know that Baron Roebuck is still a bachelor — and that the stag married a good, plain, stout doe who promptly forgot her way around the kitchen and spends all the stag's money on ruffled gowns and lace fans and things like that. And if he dares to cross her in any way, she attacks him with a wet mop. So they aren't nearly as devoted a pair as Byron Bobcat and Barbara.

As for Hollyhock Haven, the kangaroo's business continues to thrive. You can't imagine the many animals who like to get away from it all now and then!

And year in, year out, whatever the weather, you can always find the baboon at the corner of Seventh and Terrapin, selling his papers, making correct change, and replying to customers, as needed, "Thank you," "Yes," "No," "Pardon?" or "Mind your language!" Whenever the Dowager Duchess Suzanne is out of sorts she summons him and they sing together the old songs. He never fails to receive an invitation to her annual ball, but he never chooses to attend. For the rest, he enjoys reading in the papers surrounding him of venturesome mountain goats planting flags on peaks above the clouds, of walrus touring the seven seas, and even of the doings of the flower of the

realm. Then, folding the pages neatly, he returns
them to their stacks and, if the wind is cold, turns
up his collar, reheats the coffeepot, and is as con-
tented as anyone I know.